# Excuses, Excuses

## POEMS ABOUT SCHOOL

## Compiled by John Foster

Oxford University Press, Great Clarendon Street,
Oxford OX2 6DP

Oxford   New York
Athens   Auckland   Bangkok   Bogota   Bombay
Buenos Aires   Calcutta   Cape Town   Dar es Salaam
Delhi   Florence   Hong Kong   Istanbul   Karachi
Kuala Lumpur   Madras   Madrid   Melbourne
Mexico City   Nairobi   Paris   Singapore
Taipei   Tokyo   Toronto

and associated companies in
Berlin Ibadan

Oxford is a trade mark of Oxford University Press

This selection and arrangement © John Foster 1997

First published 1997

A CIP catalogue record for this book is available from the
British Library

ISBN 0 19 276150 1 (hardback)
ISBN 0 19 276151 X (paperback)

Printed and bound in Great Britain by
Biddles Ltd, Guildford and King's Lynn

# contents

❯ IN THE PLAYGROUND

❯ TEACHERS! I DON'T UNDERSTAND THEM

❯ DO WE HAVE TO WRITE A POEM ABOUT IT, MISS?

❯ TEACHER'S VERY QUIET TODAY

⟩ AND HOW WAS SCHOOL, TODAY?

# Back-to-School
# BLUES

# Back-to-School Blues

Hair's been cut. It's neat again.
Got socks and shoes on my feet again.
Saddled with a bag as new as my shoes,
I got the mean ol' back-to-school blues.

*Elizabeth Honey*

# September Shoe Rap

**De only good ting
bout back to school
is buyin new shoes
and playin de fool.**

**September here,
summer garn,
mi trainers off,
mi new shoes on!**

Mi mum say, Gial
ya playin no more,
keep bright, black shoe
from nine till four.

From nine till four
I sit in school,
but on mi way home
I forget de rules.

I run in de grass
kick up de dust
mi bright, black shoe
their shine don't last.

Mi mum see mi shoe,
she look real mean.
She get out a cloth
and make me clean.

I polish mi shoe
and they shine bright.
Me new, black shoes
make September all right.

*Chris Riley*

# Uniform

'You'll grow,' she said and that was that. No use
To argue and to sulk invited slaps.
The empty shoulders drooped, the sleeves hung
    loose —
No use — she nods and the assistant wraps.

New blazer, new school socks and all between
Designed for pea pod anonymity.
All underwear the regulation green;
Alike there's none to envy, none to pity.

At home she feasts on pins. She tacks and tucks
Takes in the generous seams and smiles at thrift.
I fidget as she fits. She tuts and clucks.
With each neat stitch she digs a deeper rift.

They'll mock me with her turnings and her hem
And laugh and know that I'm not one of them.

*Jan Dean*

# Quieter Than Snow

I went to school a day too soon
And couldn't understand
Why silence hung in the yard like sheets
Nothing to flap or spin, no creaks
Or shocks of voices, only air.

And the car park empty of teachers' cars
Only the first September leaves
Dropping like paper. No racks of bikes
No kicking legs, no fights,
No voices, laughter, anything.

Yet the door was open. My feet
Sucked down the corridor. My reflection
Walked with me past the hall.
My classroom smelt of nothing. And the silence
Rolled like thunder in my ears.

At every desk a still child stared at me
Teachers walked through walls and back again
Cupboard doors swung open, and out crept
More silent children, and still more.

They tiptoed round me
Touched me with ice-cold hands
And opened up their mouths with laughter
That was

Quieter than snow.

*Berlie Doherty*

# First Day

I still can remember
My first day at school
In that dim and distant
Dusty, chalky past.

And often I wish,
With each new September,
That my first tearful day
Had been also my last!

*John Kitching*

# I'm Telling You

**Mam said
'If you wear that skirt when you go to school
You'll look a fool
I'm telling you.'
'Go on,' I said. 'Mam,' I said. 'Let me.'**

**Mam said
'If you wear that skirt you'll look a fright
It's much too tight
I'm telling you.'
'Go on,' I said. 'Mam,' I said. 'Let me.'**

Mam said
'If you wear that skirt it'll split in two
They'll laugh at you
I'm telling you.'
'Go on,' I said. 'Mam,' I said. 'Let me.'

'Everybody's got one, Mam,' I said,
'I can't wear my old one
I wouldn't be seen dead
In that now,' I said.
'Go on,' I said. 'Mam,' I said. 'Let me.'

So I'm wearing it and
I've got to stand
And watch the others tearing round
I can't move an inch
I feel all pinched
The sides will split if I try to sit down.

I felt really great
When I came through the gate
'I like your skirt, it's really nice,
Are you playing or not?'

They didn't ask twice
They ran, and skipped, and swung,
    and jumped,
And left me standing.
On my own.

Dumped.

*Berlie Doherty*

# Latecomers

There's a special club
In our school;
The latecomers club.

They catch slow buses
From distant places,
Never have alarm-clocks,
Always have excuses,
Wonderful excuses!

In assembly,
They sit in a bunch,
Just inside the door,
Pretending not to exist.

They grow up to be;
Glib of tongue,
Never, seemingly, in the wrong;
Novelists;
Television script-writers;
Antique dealers;
Politicians.

Such are the benefits,
Of creative excuse-making.

*John Cunliffe*

# Absent

**Dear Teacher,
my body's arrived
it sits at a table
a pen in its hand
as if it is able
to think and to act
perhaps write down the answer
to the question you've asked**

**but don't let that fool you.**

**My mind is elsewhere.
My thoughts far away.**

**So apologies, teacher,
I'm not here today.**

*Bernard Young*

# Excuses, Excuses

Late again, Blenkinsopp?

What's the excuse this time?

Not my fault, sir.

Whose fault is it then?

Grandma's, sir.

Grandma's? What did she do?

She died, sir.

Died?

She's seriously dead all right, sir.

That makes four grandmothers this term, Blenkinsopp

And all on P.E. days.

I know. It's very upsetting, sir.

How many grandmothers have you got, Blenkinsopp?

Grandmothers, sir? None, sir.

You said you had four.

All dead, sir.

And what about yesterday, Blenkinsopp?

What about yesterday, sir?

You were absent yesterday.

That was the dentist, sir.

The dentist died?

No, sir. My teeth, sir.

You missed the maths test, Blenkinsopp!

I'd been looking forward to it, sir.

Right, line up for P.E.

Can't, sir.

No such word as 'can't', Blenkinsopp.

No kit, sir.

Where is it?
Home, sir.
What's it doing at home?
Not ironed, sir.
Couldn't you iron it?
Can't, sir.
Why not?
Bad hand, sir.
Who usually does it?
Grandma, sir.
Why couldn't she do it?
Dead, sir.

*Gareth Owen*

## Please Let Me Stay At Home

**Must I go to school?**
**Must I go today?**
**I'd rather stay at home,**
**or go outside and play.**

**Must I see the teachers?**
**Can't I stay in bed?**
**School just isn't any fun**
**since they made me Head.**

*Andrew Collett*

# School Is Closed Today Because...

The Geography teacher got lost
The History teacher had a date
The R.E. teacher couldn't believe it
The Cookery teacher got stuffed
The Science teacher was a physical wreck
The Art teacher got the wrong impression
The P.E. teacher was unfit for the job
The Maths teacher had divided loyalties
The Woodwork teacher took a plane
The Music teacher went flat
The English teacher was written off
The French teacher went inseine

And then we all lost our Head

*Mike Jubb*

# School Steeplechase

Copying from books 7 – 1
Copying from duplicated notes 6 – 1
Copying from board 4 – 1
Copying from best friend in test Evens
(favourite)
Understanding what gets copied 50 – 1

Jason Phipps arriving on time 20 – 1
Jason Phipps attending assembly 40 – 1
Jason Phipps remembering his homework
100 – 1
Jason Phipps getting a detention 2 – 1
(favourite)
Jason Phipps doing a detention 500 – 1

Mr Johnson bringing the right books to lesson
10 – 1
Mr Johnson remembering which group he is
teaching 20 – 1
Mr Johnson remembering to collect in
homework 50 – 1
Mr Johnson teaching the same lesson as last
week 3 – 1 (favourite)
Mr Johnson handing back books he has
marked 200 – 1

Caroline Hudson telling sir she's got a
   headache 8 – 1
Caroline Hudson visiting the nurse 5 – 1
Caroline Hudson being unable to do games 3 – 1
Caroline Hudson spending at least one lesson
   in the toilet 2 – 1 on (favourite)
Caroline Hudson arriving without her
   cosmetics bag 50 – 1

NOTE: Bets on which day the headmaster will
wear a tie that does not clash either with his
shirt or his suit must be registered by 4.00 p.m.
on the day before the one on which you are
staking money.

If, at the end of a term, the headmaster has
failed to wear a matching tie on a single day,
the accumulator will be held over until the next
term.

All bets are subject to school rules.

*David Kitchen*

# New Leaf

Today is the first day of my new book.
I've written the date
and underlined it
in red felt-tip
with a ruler
I'm going to be different
with this book.

With this book
I'm going to be good.
With this book
I'm always going to do the date like that
dead neat
with a ruler
just like Christine Robinson.

With this book
I'll be as clever as Graham Holden,
get all my sums right, be as
neat as Mark Veitch;
I'll keep my pens and pencils
in a pencil case
and never have to borrow again.

With this book
I'm going to work hard,
not talk, be different —
with this book,
not yell out, mess about,
be silly —
with this book.

With this book
I'll be grown-up, sensible,
and everyone will want me;
I'll be picked out first
like Iain Cartwright:
no one will ever laugh at me again.
Everything will be
different

with this book...

*Mick Gowar*

# I Know the Answer

Sir — sir
I've got my hand up, sir
I know the answer.
But once again the teacher
ignores my urgent plea,
that the answer to that question
has got to be — minus three.

Sir, I know the answer.
His eyes glance above my head.
Instead it's Tommy Tucker
who answers it, instead.

'Who was the first man on the moon?'
ME, sir! Me, sir! I Know! I Know!
'SIT QUIET, BOY!
Stop jumping about…
There is no need to shout.
The question, Mark, is not referred to you…
Can you give me the answer, Sue?
Clever girl — that is correct.
NOW —
Who knows where the highest mountain in
    the world is?'

Huh!
If he thinks I'm putting my hand up
he can get lost.
I won't give him the satisfaction
of telling me to sit down —
'OK, Mark — what's the answer?
Mark! — Wake up, Mark!
In which country is the highest mountain?'
Me, sir? Do you mean me, sir?
Eh! eh!
I don't know, sir.

*Pauline Omoboye*

# What It All Means

*An explanation of the*
*traditional curriculum*
*in terms we can all*
*un-der-stand.*

Today we've got History
The story of hissing
Then we've got Physics
The science of fizzing
Later is Geography
The way to go jogging
Then we've got Mew-sic
The language of moggies
Tomorrow there's Science
The study of sighing…
My favourite's Biology
The science of buying
And then there is Art
About beating and being
And finally P.E.
The time to be —
Keeping your mouth shut.

*Trevor Millum*

# Won't You Give a Better Mark?

Let me hand in my assignment
let me be a little late
never mind the quality
teacher — feel the weight

Teacher teacher teacher
don't keep me in the dark
I know you've got a grade in mind
won't you give a better mark?

Count the numbered pages
the margins neatly drawn
please overlook the fact
that the deadline's been and gone
it's got a nice conclusion
the paragraphs are neat
my granny thinks it's really good
sure kept me off the street

Teacher teacher teacher
don't keep me in the dark
I know you've got a grade in mind
won't you give a better mark?

Let me hand in my assignment
let me be a little late
never mind the quality
teacher — feel the weight!

*Trevor Millum*

1/200 Very Poor!

# There's a Frog Down the Back of the Toilet, Miss

*Pupil:* **There's a frog down the back of the toilet,**
**miss,**
**It's lodged itself under the pipe,**
**And I need to go sort of desperate, miss,**
**Do you think it is likely to bite?**

*Teacher:* **The caretaker knows of the problem,**
**He's got it in hand, never fear;**
**Just go to the toilet, and quickly,**
**Now don't hold the lesson up, dear!**

**Pupil:** There's a spider on the lamp shade above, miss,
And it stares when you sit on the seat,
And I'm kind of scared it might fall, miss,
And I don't mean on to my feet!

**Teacher:** I'm sure there is no need to worry,
Spiders are harmless and small,
I think an attack is unlikely,
Go now, child, or don't go at all!

**Pupil:** But there's a wasp flying round the cistern, miss,
It's buzzing about to and fro,
And I'd sort of feel quite exposed, miss,
Just sitting in wait down below.

**Teacher:** I have no more time for your stories,
But I see that you've started to dance
From one leg on to the other,
So go now, this is your last chance!

There's a Frog Down the Back of the Toilet, Miss

*Teacher:* **What took you so long in the toilet, child?**
**You've missed half an hour of science;**
**Your excuse had better convince me**
**Or I'll punish your blatant defiance!**

*Pupil:* **Well, while I sat on the toilet, miss,**
**The wasp got caught in the web,**
**The spider had spun just above, miss,**
**It was almost touching my head!**

**So I grabbed up my trousers quite smartish,**
**miss,**
**And got ready to leave pretty quick,**
**When I noticed my trousers were croaking,**
**miss,**
**And I started to feel sort of sick.**

**And as I stood still in the corner, miss,**
**My trousers were leaping about,**
**And I was too frightened to move, miss,**
**Too frightened even to shout!**

**Then out of the top of my trousers, miss,**
**A little frog struggled and jumped**
**Up to the spider and wasp, miss,**
**He swallowed them both in one lump.**

Then SPLASH! the frog landed in water, miss,
He swam around having great fun,
With legs hanging out of his mouth, miss,
It was just like *Wildlife on One*!

Then I flushed him away down the loo, miss,
He swam with the flow, without pain,
I expect he'll escape very quickly, miss,
When he comes to the end of the drain.

Teacher:  Your tale is less than convincing,
You'll stay in at lunch for a week;
And unless you can tell me the truth, dear,
Please just don't bother to speak!

*ENTER CARETAKER*

Caretaker:  The boys' toilets are out of order,
I hope no one's playing a joke,
There's some sort of blockage to sort out,
A blockage that happens to croak!

*Coral Rumble*

# I Was Mucking About In Class

I was mucking about in class

Mr Brown said,
Get out and take your chair with me
I suppose he *meant* to say
Take your chair with you
so Dave said,
Yeah — you heard what he said
    get out and take my chair with him
so Ken said,
Yeah — get out and take his chair with me
so I said to Mr Brown
Yessir — shall I take our chair with you, sir?

Wow
That meant **BIG TROUBLE**

*Michael Rosen*

# 'What Are You Doing Out Here?'

Nice of you to ask, sir.
Thoughtful of you to think.
To even give me a glance, sir
Is a great encouragement.

Why I'm standing in the corridor?
That's what you want to know.
I've been sent out to cool my heels, sir
(Not that they were aglow).

I don't know exactly why, sir.
It might be because I was fighting
And I had a fit of the giggles
When I should've been quietly writing.

Oh…I did pull Jackie's hair, sir
But not really very hard
And she kicked me on the shin, sir
(A fact that's been ignored).

I'll see you after school, sir.
How kind of you to invite me.
Yes, we'll have one of our chats, sir.
No, I don't take this matter lightly.

*Bernard Young*

# You're Dead

If you copy from a friend
You're dead,
If you give the truth a bend
You're dead,
If you run instead of walk
Or shout instead of talk
You're dead,
You're dead;

If you forget your pencil case
You're dead,
If you make a funny face
You're dead,
If your pages are all blotchy
Your teacher will go potty,
You're dead,
You're dead;

If you walk over the grass
You're dead,
If you pick your nose in class
You're dead,
If your reading book gets lost
You'll have to pay the cost,
You're dead,
You're dead;

If you're talking at the back
You're dead,
If your finger nails are black

You're dead,
If you're late in your arriving
Not much chance of your surviving
You're dead,
You're dead;

If you fail the tables test
You're dead,
If you take a little rest
You're dead,
If your games kit's being washed
Or your topic's sort of squashed,
You're dead,
You're dead;

If you jump the dinner queue
You're dead,
If your name's scratched on the loo
You're dead,
If your homework is in late
Then you'll have to meet your fate,
You're dead,
You're dead;

If you're sent to see the head
You're dead,
If his face goes kind of red
You're dead,
If he reaches for the phone
And makes contact with your home...

YOU'RE DEAD!

*Coral Rumble*

# The Secret Notes of D.5.

*(written on a piece of paper towel)*

**To Dalinda,**

Meet me at playtime behind
the gardener's shed.
And don't tell anyone,
or you're
dead!

**From
Mickey Hamsterhead**

*(written on a scrap of tracing paper)*

**Mickey,**

You nit!
Are you a Norman
or just thick?
Meet <u>you</u>?
No way! You make me
sick!

**Dalinda Parrotstick**

(on a pink page from a memo pad)

**Dearest Gaz,**

Well, are you coming to my party, or not?
It's tonight and Jane wants to meet you there.
All right?

Love,
from
X  Marie Mittymite

(on a sheet ripped from a 'Rough Book')

**To Marie,**

Look,
leave it out!
I <u>hate</u> parties
and I don't like Jane.
<u>All</u> girls are hopeless
and she's a real
pain.

Gaz Pulldechain

(on the back of an Old Valentine card)

**To Morag,**

I know it's July and this card is really late, but will you go out with me and be my date?

**From**

**Guess who?**

(P.S. My name rhymes with 'blue')

**To Robert Kickapoo (I know it's you!),**

I can't stand boys who

always shout

'Hi!' and 'Yo!'

And you pick your nose!

So,

my answer is

NO!

Get Lost!

✳

**Morag Snow**

(on a sheet of lined writing paper)

*(written on the blackboard)*

## To class D.5,

Stop sending notes.
I'm getting fed-up
with finding
such silly stuff.
Get on with your work!
No more notes!
Enough
is enough!

### From
### Mrs Dillyduff

*Wes Magee*

# Teacher's Pet

Teacher's pet is a squirt and a soppy-clogs,
and teacher's pet is a sneak,
and teacher's pet gets some kind of special job
every day of the week,
and teacher's pet gets good marks for everything,
and teacher's pet is a bore,
and teacher's pet is sickly and simpery,
and goody-girly to the core.

And me, I sit in the back row for every class,
and me, I tell rude jokes,
and me, I don't get good marks for anything,
and me, I'm one of the blokes —
so why do I feel stupid and stuttery
and what's this pain I get,
that makes me go all floozy and fluttery —
at a smile from teacher's pet?

*Rowena Somerville*

# Thirteen Questions You Should Be Prepared To Answer If You Lose Your Ears At School

Are they clearly named?
When did you notice they were missing?
Were they fixed on properly?
What colour are they?
What size?
Have you looked in the playground?
Did you take them off for P.E.?
Could somebody else have picked them up by mistake?
Have you felt behind the radiators?
Did you lend them to anybody?
Have you searched the bottom of your bag?
Does the person you sit next to have a similar pair?
Are you sure you brought them to school this morning?

*John Coldwell*

# The Games Lesson

The field was large, and round the edge
Were bushes, trees and long grass where
Imagination stirred.

Miss Evans said, Now find a space
Away from anybody else.
We took her at her word.

In all directions we dispersed
To find our space and be alone
Where distances were blurred.

Miss Evans, helpless, watched us go
And called to us, Come back at once,
This really is absurd.

But we were far away by then
And learning from the outside world
Where her voice was not heard.

And hundreds of Miss Evanses
Still peer shortsighted after us,
Uncertain what occurred.

*Sandy Brownjohn*

# Team Spirit

*Oh no, not him, sir. He's no good.*
I didn't ask to join their team.
I try, but I run out of steam
And let them down again. Dead wood.

The joys of sporting brotherhood
Are not for me. I spoil their scheme.
*Oh no, not him, sir. He's no good.*
I didn't ask to join their team.

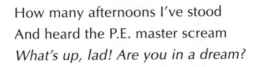

How many afternoons I've stood
And heard the P.E. master scream
*What's up, lad! Are you in a dream?*

I wish I was. I wish I could.
But this is real and I'm no good
And Hell is being in a team.

*Wendy Cope*

# The Carol Singer

They tell me my singing is painful —
I sound like the twanging of wire,
Or finger nails scratching a blackboard . . .
And now I've been sacked from the choir.

They told me I shouldn't go singing;
They told me that crime wouldn't pay;
But look — I've collected a fortune
In bribes . . . just to keep me away.

*Clare Bevan*

# In the Playground

# In the Playground

Philip is spinning
Patrick's pushing — Kuldip's kicking
Russell's rushing

Rachel's running
Tina's tripping — Helen's hopping
Sarah's skipping

Chris is chasing
Claire is dodging — Ben is bumping
James is jogging

Simon's standing
Steven's staring — Estelle's eating
Samantha's sharing

Sukvinder's shoving
Helen's hugging — LeRoy's leading
Tasmin's tugging

Tracey

End of play!

*Maggie Holmes*

# Winter Break

Katie's lucky.
She's been told
to stay inside at playtime.
I wish I had a cold!

Ahmed's lucky.
He got only two
in Monday's spelling test.
I wish I had to stay inside
to learn the rest!

Our teacher's lucky.
At playtime Mr Mould
drinks coffee in the staffroom.
I wish I was old!

Each day's the same.
The sky is grey,
the wind is cold
but *still* they say
'Off you go now,
out to play!'

It's never *me* who's told
to stay inside.
I hate it,
yes, I *hate* it,
stuck out here in the cold!

*Judith Nicholls*

# Playground Haiku

Everyone says our
playground is overcrowded
but I feel lonely.


*Helen Dunmore*

# New Boy

He stood alone in the playground
Scuffed his shoes and stared at the ground
He'd come half-way through term from the
    Catholic school
On the other side of town.

He'd a brand new blazer and cap on
Polished shoes and neatly cut hair
Blew on his fists, looked up and half smiled
Pretending he didn't care.

And I remembered when I'd been new
And no one had spoken to me
I'd almost cried as I stood alone
Hiding my misery.

Heart said I should go over
Share a joke or play the fool
But I was scared of looking stupid
In front of the rest of the school.

At break someone said they'd seen him
Crying in the Geography Test
And when he came out they pointed and
    laughed
And I laughed along with the rest.

In my dreams I'd always stood alone
Believing I was the best
But in the cold playground of everyday life
I was no better than the rest.

*Gareth Owen*

# Different

She was new here and
different; talked different
wore strange clothes

and the food
in her packed lunch
— bizarre!

Everything about her
different
from them.

But some of them
big enough
to make space for her.

Some big enough to realize
that the world is
a place of differences

and that's its richness
the way it was made
— to survive.

*Joan Poulson*

# The Fight

There's a fight on the playground today —
  Two big boys from Mr Magee's
Are knocking the daylights out of each other
  Under the trees.

The girls are silent and staring
  And Clare whispers 'Stop it, Paul'
As the fighting gets wilder, and feet jab out
  And fingers maul.

I watch, and I'm glad it's not Joe
  And me in that horrible space —
Not my stomach winded, not my nose bleeding,
  Not my burning face.

The sky is bright. Two planes fly
  Out from the base, while one
Boy holds the other down with his knee
  And breathes 'You done?'

There's a fight on the playground today —
  Paul Topple from Mr Magee's
Is crushing the daylights out of John Randall
  Under the trees.

*Fred Sedgwick*

# School Bully

*Give in!* your classmates said. *Give in!* — sharing
Your pain almost — as his knees sent glass
Slivers burning like black
Stars up
Your spine, and very close to your watering eye,
The many-sided worlds of grit
Shone in the playtime sun.
As he held you
Face down
Hard on the ground, you heard the skipping, wall-
Ball-bouncing voices that seemed now
So far from this mad world
Behind the bike
Shed. *No!*
You said to the urgent voices that
Were fearful of this lock, this jam of wills.

Yet somehow pain and fear
Went far away
And joined
The other little voices in the sun;
And as his face came closer and
You smelt his foul tobacco-
Stained breath hit
You like
An old, sad room, full of dark secrets, then
You knew you'd won, and as his hands
Like hard white spiders searched

You for a door
To let
More pain come crashing in, you smiled through
    tears,
Sensing his awful fear and loss
As, eternities away, the bell tolled.

*Mike Harding*

# Shoot the Messenger!

On playground duty, while sipping her tea,
Miss Martin told us stories.

'Long ago,' she said,'If he brought bad news,
they used to shoot the messenger.

This bringer of bad tidings,
message hidden, horse hard-ridden
would burst upon the scene
with news of some huge defeat
in battle.

And the first response would be,
pretend it hadn't happened,
make out they hadn't heard,
shoot the messenger,
forget his words.'

We listened, open-mouthed.
Miss Martin was smart,
her story must be true.

'Now,' she said, 'I've a job for someone.

Who wants to go to the staffroom
to tell the teachers
it's end of break?'

*Brian Moses*

# It's Cold

Dem teacher in di staffroom
Dem a lock up di door.
Dem teacher in di staffroom,
You'd tink it a war.

Dem teacher in di staffroom
Dem a drink dem tea.
Dem are looking tru di window
An laughin at we.

Outside in di playgroun,
Dem pupil a freezin.
Rubbin dem hans,
Coughin and wheezin.

Dem pupil a chant,
'Let we in, we cold.'
Dem teacher, dem a shout,
'You do as you told.'

Dem pips a soun,
It a time fi go in.
Wait a minute, man.
It start a snowin.

Now di snow quickly form
A layer of white.
And what do you know?
A snowball fight.

Dem snowballs is flyin
All over di place.
An one a dem a hit
A teacher in di face.

Now a strange ting happen
A we haf fi grin.
Dem teacher making snowballs
And joining in.

Now di snow start a flyin
Tru di air,
Splashing on your coat;
On your legs; in your hair.

Before too long
We all soaking wet.
And pupil an teacher say,
'Best lesson yet.'

*John Coldwell*

# Morning Break

**Eleven o'clock:**
**seagulls noisy as children**
**pick up crisps from the empty playground.**

*Adrian Henri*

# TEACHERS!

# I don't understand them .....

# Teachers

Teachers!
I don't understand them.

They say:
>    When you hand in your work,
>    Make sure it's neat and tidy.
Then they mess it up
By scribbling illegible comments
All over it in red ink.

They say:
>    Don't interrupt when I'm talking.
>    Put your hand up
>    And wait until I've finished.
But if they've got something to say,
They clap their hands
And stop your discussions in mid-sentence.

They say:
    Always plan your writing.
    Take your time. Think it through
    And do a rough draft.
Then they sit you in an examination hall
And ask you to write an essay
On one of six topics —
None of which interests you —
In an hour and a quarter.

They say:
    All work and no play
    Makes Jill a dull girl.
    Make sure you allow yourself
    Time off from your studies
    To relax and enjoy yourself.
Then, when you don't hand
Your homework in on time,
Because you took their advice,
They keep you in after school.

Teachers!
I don't understand them.

*John Foster*

# The Drama Teacher

*I'm going through the jungle,*
*Follow me,* he said
*Hear the rhinos rumble,*
I think he's off his head.

*We're dressed in our pyjamas —*
*Just off the* Titanic.
I think he's gone bananas
*OK, kids — don't panic.*

*We're soldiers in a Roman fort*
*Wearing funny hats.*
This proves what we have always thought:
He's absolutely bats.

*Mike Kivi*

# Shorthand

Our English teacher's
punctuated.

Our Music teacher's
crotchet.

Our Science teacher's
fractal.

But our Humanities teacher's
tropic.

*Joan Poulson*

# Mr Body, the Head

Our Head, Mr Body, is six feet tall,
he's always on his toes and has a heart of gold.
He has a finger in every pie
and a chip on his shoulder.

He doesn't stand for any cheek
and so we don't give him any lip
— and we don't talk back.

Mr Body knows when we're pulling his leg
and he says, 'Hold your tongue,
just you knuckle under and toe the line.
I want no underhand tricks here!'

He says our new school
cost an arm and a leg to build.
He had to fight for it tooth and nail.

Mr Body says he shoulders the burden of
    responsibility
and ends up doing the work of four people.
That must make him a forehead.

*John Rice*

# My Headmistress

My headmistress
is a maniac.

She uses
the wrong side
of the road.

She parks
where she shouldn't.

She never signals.

I sometimes think
she shouldn't be allowed out
on that skateboard.

*Bernard Young*

# Headteachers . . . at Assembly

**This one**
jangles a bunch of keys in his pocket,
hates bad behaviour, talks about 'serious cases'.
He stands very close to the front row and once,
during prayers, a boy untied his shoe laces.
The Head turned, tripped, fell to the floor.
There were smiles on all our faces.

**This one**
is a Great Lady. She wears a knitted shawl
and is always at the hairdresser's: hates muck.
When she holds up items of Lost Property
she shudders in horror and says, 'Yeeeeerh! Yuk!'
Socks, shorts or underpants are *never* claimed.
She makes noises like a hen . . . cluck, cluck, cluck.

**This one**
wears snazzy ties and toeless sandals.
He has nicknames for everyone . . . like Grub, Wombat,
   or Mad.
If you drop your recorder he'll say,
'You know, that's a hanging offence, lad!'
He winks, does funny walks, and his jokes
are the world's worst . . . really, really bad.

This one
paces up and down like a caged tigress,
her face red as an overripe tomato.
She goes crazy if she hears a cough
and shouts, 'No coughing! *No coughing!* NO!'
But someone coughs, then another: an avalanche of
coughs.
Her nose turns crimson and starts to glow.

This one
we call Hitler. He rants and raves every day
and his hair is slicked down flat on his head.
His suits are black, his shoes glassy black,
but his eyes have a suspicious tinge of red.
He fancies our Miss Squash; tells us to rise early,
clean our teeth, and make the bed.

This one
is everyone's friend, knows all our names
and never forgets a birthday.
She whispers so softly that no one can hear a word!
Her hair and eyebrows are totally grey.
When I lost a pound coin she replaced it!
I'll remember that to my dying day.

*Wes Magee*

# Yaketty-Yak

Why does my teacher talk all the time?
The talking begins at a minute to nine
When we're outside the door standing neatly in line.
    Yaketty-yaketty-yak

Each lesson begins with a speech from the floor,
We think he has finished but then comes some more;
One thing is clear — he knows how to jaw.
    Yaketty-yaketty-yak

Then come the questions as rapid as rain.
Why does he ask them again and again?
When I don't understand, why won't he explain?
    Yaketty-yaketty-yak

Our room has computers, there's no sign of chalk,
Just twenty-eight pupils forbidden to talk,
With a teacher who watches us just like a hawk.
    Yaketty-yaketty-yak

'You will listen to me. You will not answer back.
Write neatly; in silence; in biro; in black.
No chewing, no talking and no one will slack.'
    Yaketty-yaketty-yak

When the kids stay at home (I'm not really complaining),
The days when the teachers go off for their training,
Who stands at the front and does all the explaining?
    Yaketty-yaketty-yak

But listen to this — it's a kind of confession —
When I grow up and work in my chosen profession,
A teacher I'll be, and I'll speak with expression,
    Yaketty-yaketty-yak

*Jack Ousbey*

# Day Closure

We had a day closure on Monday
and I spent the morning in bed,
but the teachers went in as usual
and someone taught them instead.

And I thought of them all in the classroom,
stuck to their seats in rows,
some of them sucking pen lids,
Head Teacher scratching his nose.

Perhaps it's a bit like an M.O.T.
to check if teachers still know
the dates of our kings and queens
or the capital of so and so.

Perhaps they had tables and spellings,
did the Head give them marks out of ten?
And then, if they got any wrong,
did he make them learn them again?

I thought of them out at break time
playing football or kiss chase or tag,
picking up teams in the playground
or scoffing crisps from a bag.

If I had been a fly on the wall,
I might have watched while they slaved,
I'd have seen who asked silly questions
or if anyone misbehaved.

I thought of them all going home,
crossing the road to their mums.
They looked very grim the next day.
It couldn't have been much fun.

*Brian Moses*

# Strict

Maybe you think you have a teacher
who's really strict
maybe you know a really strict teacher.
But when I was at school
we had a teacher who was so strict
you weren't allowed to breathe in her lessons.
That's true, we weren't allowed to breathe.
It was really hard to get through
a whole day without breathing.
Lips tightly shut.
Face going red.
Eyeballs popping out.
She'd go round the class glaring at us
and then she'd suddenly catch sight of one of us
and she'd yell
NO BREATHING, DO YOU HEAR ME? NO BREATHING.
And you had to stop breathing right away.
The naughty ones used to try and take quick secret breaths
under the table.
They'd duck down where she couldn't see them
snatch a quick breath and come back up
with their mouth shut tight.
Then someone would say,
'Excuse me, miss, can I go outside and do some breathing?'
And she'd say
'WHAT? CAN'T YOU WAIT? YOU'VE HAD ALL PLAYTIME
TO BREATHE, HAVEN'T YOU?'
And then she'd ask someone a question

like, 'Where's Tibet?'
and someone'd put up their hand and say
'Er . . . it's —'
and she'd be right in there with:
'YOU'RE BREATHING! I SAW YOU BREATHE.'
'I wasn't, miss, really I wasn't.'
'WELL, YOU ARE NOW, AREN'T YOU?'
It was terrible.
She was so strict . . .

*Michael Rosen*

# On Current Corporal Punishment

**There was a young teacher from Staines**
**Who simply hated the use of Canes;**
    **He had other controls**
    **For deviant souls,**
**Such as plugging them into the Mains.**

*David R. Morgan*

# A Schoolmistress Called Binks Lies Here

A schoolmistress called Binks lies here.
She held her own for twenty year.
She pleaded, biffed, said: 'I'm your friend.'
But children got her in the end.

*Roy Fuller*

# Miss Rodd

**Our teacher's name was Miss Rodd.**
**She spoiled us good and proper,**
**Taught us what Authority meant.**
**With a thwack here and a hundred lines there,**
**She never spared the child.**
**When we left school,**
**We were the first to rebel.**

*John Foster*

# Our Teacher's Voice

Our teacher lost his voice today.
We said we'd look for it,
poking into cupboards
and under tables till he croaked:
'Will you stop all this silliness
and go and get on with your work.'

'Have you really lost your voice?'
we asked, till someone tried
the same daft question once
too often, and he slapped down
a metre rule so hard that it broke.

Then he wrote what we had to do
on the board, we pretended
we didn't understand, then laughed
as he tried to explain,
voice reduced to whispering,
eyes darting this way and that.

At three thirty we bundled off home.
'Our teacher lost his voice today,'
we called out, to anyone who'd listen.

'I'm not surprised,' Mum said.
'That must have been rotten,
knowing you lot!'

'What do you mean, knowing us lot?' we said.
'He yells too much,
he wore it out!'

But if he's not there tomorrow,
the Head might take our class
and he's been known to cuff and clout.
Let's hope our teacher's voice
is back to a shout.

*Brian Moses*

# Artificial Intelligence Test

There are twelve robots in my class
And I don't think it's fair
It makes exams a total farce
The metal monsters always pass
It's more than I can bear

Humans have to swot and sweat
To keep up with their peers
Each robot is the teacher's pet
And yet I've seen them fume and fret
And very close to tears

Sometimes their motor drive goes dead
And memory banks are fused
This is our chance to get ahead
To get good marks in our co-ed
While robots are excused

But artificial intelligence
Is where the future lies
(No pranks, no disobedience)
Silicon omnipotence
Our teacher prophesies

When she speaks her sensors flash
Antennae twitch and sway:
'Sit up straight, you carbon trash
Your homework's utter balderdash
Now robots rule, OK!'

What can we say, what can we do?
In this brave new age
We're the smartass human crew
Who engineered the android coup
And built ourselves a cage

*Paul Sidey*

# The Head's Hideout

The Head crouched in his hideout
Beneath a dustbin lid.
'I want to see,' he muttered,
'No teacher and no kid,

No parent, no inspector,
Never a district nurse,
And, please, not one school dinner:
The things are getting worse!'

All morning, as the phone rang,
He hid away. Instead:
'The Head is in the dustbin,'
The secretary said.

'The *Head* is in the *dustbin?*'
'Yes, he'll be there all day.
He likes sometimes to manage
A little getaway.

Last year he went to Holland.
Next year he's off to France.
Today he's in the dustbin.
You have to take your chance.'

The Head sprang from the garbage
As end-of-school came round.
He cried, 'That's quite the nastiest
Hideaway I've found!

I think I'll stick to teachers
And kids and parents too.
It's just sometimes I've had enough.'
Don't blame him. Do you?

*Kit Wright*

# Do We Have to Write a Poem About It, Miss

# What Do Teachers Dream Of?

What do teachers dream of,
In mountains and in lowlands?
They dream of exclamation marks,
Full stops and semi-colons!

*Colin West*

# I Am a Question Mark

I am a question mark.
I sit on the keyboard
Waiting to be of service
In investigations and interrogations.
I help people with their enquiries.
If you're lost,
I can help you find the way.
If you're puzzled,
I can help you search for a solution.
If there's anything you need to know,
Just ask
And I'll show
That an answer's expected.

*John Foster*

# Creative Writing

My story on Monday began:

> *Mountainous seas crashed on the cliffs,*
> *And the desolate land grew wetter...*

The teacher wrote a little note: *Remember the capital letter!*

My poem on Tuesday began:

> *Red tongues of fire,*
> *Licked higher and higher*
> *From smoking Etna's top ...*

The teacher wrote a little note: *Where is your full stop?*

My story on Wednesday began:

> *Through the lonely, pine-scented wood*
> *There twists a hidden path ...*

The teacher wrote a little note: *Start a paragraph!*

My poem on Thursday began:
> *The trembling child,*
> *Eyes dark and wild,*
> *Frozen midst the fighting . . .*

The teacher wrote a little note: *Take care untidy writing!*

My story on Friday began:
> *The boxer bruised and bloody lay,*
> *His eye half closed and swollen*

The teacher wrote a little note: *Use a semi colon!*

Next Monday my story will begin:
> *Once upon a time . . .*

*Gervase Phinn*

# Do We *Have* to Write a Poem About It, Miss?

There was a freezing storm outside.
So our teacher decides to send us into the playground
to feel it.
We felt it.
And when we got back inside she said,
'Now write a poem about the wind.'
So here it is:

> *Blow the wind!*

We hatched some eggs in our classroom.
But it wasn't enough for her
just to let us watch the chicks
to enjoy them and talk about them. Oh no.
'Now write a poem about chickens.'
So here it is:

> *Stuff chickens!*

I like short poems.

Here's the one about our visit
to the man who keeps bees: *Buzz off!*
The policeman: *Not much cop.*
Tadpoles turning into frogs: *Hop it!*
The grasshopper: *It's not cricket.*
Going on a journey: *Get lost!*
Out in the rain: *I've wet myself.*

**The school doctor:** *She makes me sick!*
**Helping each other:** *Do me a favour!*
**The visiting juggler:** *Makes me want to throw up!*
**At the seaside:** *The sea waves,*
*So I wave back.*

**Hey! I think I'm getting the hang of this writing lark.**

*Mike Jubb*

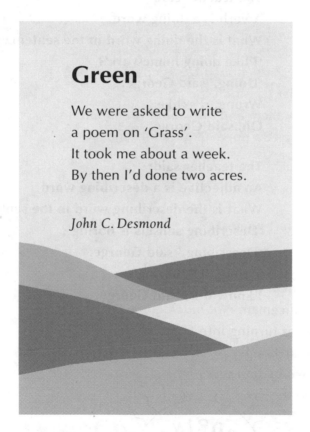

# Green

We were asked to write
a poem on 'Grass'.
It took me about a week.
By then I'd done two acres.

*John C. Desmond*

# Grammar

The teacher said:
A noun is a naming word.
What is the naming word in the sentence:
'He named the ship *Lusitania*'?
'Named,' said George.
Wrong, it's 'ship'.
Oh, said George.

The teacher said:
A verb is a doing word.
What is the doing word in the sentence:
'I like doing homework'?
'Doing,' said George.
Wrong, it's 'like'.
Oh, said George.

The teacher said:
An adjective is a describing word.
What is the describing word in the sentence:
'Describing sunsets is boring'?
'Describing,' said George.
Wrong, it's 'boring'.
I know it is, said George.

*Michael Rosen*

# Marked

My English book's full —
It's dead, deceased —
Curled at the corners,
The cover creased.
Name and Subject
Just a blur;
Inside, slaved over
By me and sir.
He says, 'Look it through
From front to back.
Ask yourself:
Is it good — or slack?'
So I flip it through
From front to back
And read the red
Below the black:

Quite a good start.
Take more care.
Disappointing.
Only fair.
Not your best.
This is careless stuff.
You simply don't
Try hard enough.

And that's not true —
I really tried.
There's plenty more
In red beside:
Remarks that cut
Worse than a knife.
This marking's left me
Marked for life.

*Eric Finney*

# The Explanation

From my thicket's safe twilight
I have emerged timorously
seeking an explanation
for multiplying fractions.
This is the third time
my teacher has explained —
once to the class,
twice to me alone.
Each time I see the figures
not the links between them:
random clouds glimpsed
through bracken fronds.
Only this time
I have learned to nod
when his voice rises
and his hand lies still.
*...and then you cancel*
*this one. Do you see?*
I nod. I see,
but do not understand.

The pencil moves again.
I watch the fingers
backed with furzy hair
flex and move and stop.
*Do you understand it now?*
I nod as instinct
draws me back brainfrozen
into tangled bush.
After this explanation
I understand the flash
of fear, the white
glare of failure.
In class I will
copy answers,
learn to look wise,
keep my hand down,
lie doggo in the undergrowth.

*Barrie Wade*

# Please Read!

'You, please read!' the teacher said,
Pointing her finger at me.
The blood rushed up to my face
And my body began to freeze.

Oh, how I hated standing up
To read in front of the class.
I swallowed and coughed and shuffled about
And began to read very fast.

I mumbled and stumbled and whispered and
squeaked;
'Speak up!' thundered teacher to me.
I tried to make my voice boom out,
But it faded, pathetically.

'Another verse!' the teacher called,
As quickly I went to sit down.
I'd lost my place on the page by then
And felt such a clumsy clown.

The words kept dancing all over the page,
My heartbeat thumped in my head,
The boys behind me sniggered;
Oh, I wished that I were dead.

At last she commanded, 'Right, that will do,'
And I sat down fast with relief.
But in my haste I knocked over the book
And a bottle of ink came to grief.

'Good heavens, girl, what's the matter with you?'
She frowned, with a withering look,
'All I asked you to do was stand up and read
A page from your poetry book.'

*Maggie Holmes*

# Fox

Midwinter, mid-morning
Of a dark-grey day.
Outside snow settles
On a playground
Where we won't be allowed to play.

We're inside, in the warm
Classroom, listening
As miss reads poems . . .
One where a fox
Comes trotting, green eyes glistening,

Out of a midnight forest,
Into a poet's mind.
I see it clearly:
Sharp ears, long snout,
Red, soft fur stirring in the wind . . .

The poem's called *The Thought-Fox.*
Miss says it's a great
Way of capturing
A fox in words.
*Then I see it at the school gate,*

There, where the bushes hide
Overflowing bins.
I hold my breath, stare
Through the window
And feel a tingling in my skin.

The fox breathes steam. It's real,
A city creature
Forced out in daylight
To scavenge scraps.
It stands proud, beyond our teacher.

'Miss!' someone hisses. It's
By the gate, just look!'
But miss keeps reading,
Takes no notice,
Eyes fixed on the pages of her book.

Whispers grow, till at last
Miss crossly turns, peers
Where we're all pointing,
But she's too late.
A swift red shadow disappears.

Miss tuts, and blames our strong
Imaginations,
The poem's power.
She looks away,
Happy with her explanation,

Picks up where she left off . . .
But the trail is cold.
Outside snow settles,
Slowly covers
The tracks that show a fox was bold.

*Tony Bradman*

# Signs of Education

This way to
the back of the
bicycle sheds

Headmaster's tyres
have been let down
again: high sensitivity
suspension area

Warning: Mr Timmin's
Bike Maintenance Group have
been left unsupervised again

In this area,
dinner ladies have
been replaced by
mounted police

Number of supply teachers
known to have resigned as
a consequence of
teaching 10F

Marks last positive
sighting of school gates
shortly prior to 10F's
C.D.T. project

Teacher in car
seeking revenge
on 10F

Geography field trip
with Miss Fothergill

Geography field group
following Miss Fothergill's
map and instructions

Danger: this is
where the year nines
mugged Father Christmas
last year

End of term

*David Kitchen*

# Summer

I can hear grass growing
through this open window.
It doesn't have to know
about multiplication;
it just gets on with it.
I wish it would speed up
and swallow this room;
make it a jungle where
we could hunt for adders
to help with our maths,
or those large snakes
to tell us about
Pythonagoras' theorem.

*John C. Desmond*

Teacher's
Very *Quiet*
Today

# On Monday Morning

There's been a break-in
   down at the school
and our classroom's been wrecked
   by some stupid fool.

The police have arrived
   all smart-dressed and slim.
Our teachers are cross.
   The Head's looking grim.

Six windows are broken.
   We must wait in the Hall.
But there's nothing to do
   so we stare at the wall.

They've paint-sprayed the desks,
   thrown books on the floor,
snapped off all our plants
   and kicked in the door.

That room was our home,
   we worked there with pride
but now it's a wreck
   and we can't go inside.

Detectives are searching
   for footprints and clues.
*We're* still in our coats
   and full of the blues.

One girl's heard a rumour,
   she gives name and address.
Now the caretaker's here
   to clear up the mess.

Much later that morning
   we're back in our place.
Card over the windows.
   It's all a disgrace.

The vandals stole pens.
   Our hamster's not fed.
There's pain in my heart,
   an ache in my head.

There's been a break-in
   down at the school
and our classroom's been wrecked
   by some stupid fool.

*Wes Magee*

# Teacher's Very Quiet Today

Teacher's very quiet today,
hasn't shouted once
but just let us get on with things
in a casual sort of way.

Several times I caught her gaze
but I wasn't even noticed.
Teacher looks preoccupied
like something's weighing heavy on her
  mind.

I don't know what it is
but I think I've seen that look before.
The expression seems familiar
but not in school.

It's more like the look Dad had
when he crashed his new car
or Mum when she found out
Auntie Jo was ill.

Teacher's very quiet today,
hasn't shouted once
but just let us get on with things
in a casual sort of way.

*Paul Cookson*

# Donna Didn't Come Back

Donna didn't come back
on Monday.
We all knew
what had happened
and found we couldn't remember
her face before
her crutches and fallen-out hair.
No one ever talked
about what she had
or what she was.

Even so,
and despite her eyes
which said I'm tired
I give up,
we all expected her
to come in that door
sit down to maths
and pretend
the world was still
OK.

*Steve Bowkett*

# No Ordinary Day

It was the saddest day
we had ever known.
No pushing or shoving,
everyone unusually
  well-behaved.

Assembly, no teachers,
just us listening, the Head
holding back tears, trying
to tell us how she felt about
  the accident.

Playtime, but nobody
played. We whispered,
watching the empty road,
where no one walked this
  summer morning.

The village held its breath.
We stood by the gate, cooks,
cleaners, caretaker, teachers,
children. We waited together
  in silence.

Then, 'He's coming! Adrian's
coming!' one of the little ones
called. Glittering like glass,
a long black car inched
    round the corner.

In the back, a small coffin,
buried under a mound of
flowers. Then came the cars
full of familiar people in
    unfamiliar black.

They slid past the school.
'A five-minute run-around,
then inside!' the duty teacher
said. Released, we tumbled on
    to the grass.

The day struggled back to
nearly-normal. At home-time,
parents grabbed our hands
and the ice-cream van had
    few customers.

*Moira Andrew*

# Duncan Gets Expelled

There are three big boys from primary seven
who wait at the main school gate with stones
in their teeth and names in their pockets.
Every day the three big boys are waiting.
'There she is. Into her, boys. Hey, Sambo.'

I dread the bell ringing, and the walk home.
My best friend is scared of them and runs off.
Some days they shove a mud pie into my mouth.
'That's what you should eat,' and make me eat it.
Then they all look in my mouth, prodding a stick.

I'm always hoping we get detention.
I'd love to write 'I will be better' 400 times.
The things I do? I pull Agnes MacNamara's hair.
Or put a ruler under Rhona's bum and ping it back
till she screams; or I make myself sick in the toilet.

Until the day the headmaster pulls me out,
asking all about the three big boys.
I'm scared to open my mouth.
But he says, 'You can tell me, is it true?'
So out it comes, making me eat the mud pies.

Two of them got lines for the whole of May.
But he got expelled, that Duncan MacKay.

*Jackie Kay*

# Congratulations Assembly

**At the end of the congratulations assembly**
**when one by one**
**the whole school had climbed on to the platform,**
**the merit badge winners,**
**the swimming certificates,**
**the improved spellers,**
**the birthday boys and girls,**
**the reformed delinquents,**
**the teachers,**
**the caretaker's grandmother**
**and the crossing lady's dog,**
**a stray ray of sunshine**
**popped through a window,**
**illuminated where I sat**
**and squashed me.**

*Brian Morse*

# Not Wagging But Towning

My new school calls it 'towning' or else
   'playing hookey'
but really it's the same as 'skiving off' or
   'wagging school'

except I've found it's less like puppies on the
   loose
than stray old dogs with tails hung down

slinking shamefaced down lonely streets
and miserable with nowhere safe to go.

I know there's not a single welcome mat
in brick and concrete and these frozen faces.

I hate this town now more than boys who tease
and teachers who don't seem to care or even
   see

that all I want is to be let to play
and run along with other folk around

not cold and pushed out to the utmost fringe
like some unwanted mongrel booted down a
   yard.

*Barrie Wade*

# The Boy

I am the boy in the playground,
   The boy who stands by the wall,
The boy that no one likes much,
   And some don't like at all.

I am the boy with a problem,
   The boy at the back of the class,
The boy who finds it hard to read,
   And tests too hard to pass.

I am the boy no one plays with,
   The boy who walks home alone,
The boy that some wish didn't exist,
   And who wishes his heart was stone.

I am the boy with no future,
   The boy with a difficult past,
The boy who ought to be first in the queue,
   And somehow is always . . . the last.

*Tony Bradman*

# Slow Jeanie

There is this girl in my class called Jeanie.
She doesn't play with anybody much.
She is still on early readers.
Sometimes she does good pictures,
but she is not careful.
Sometimes she wears the same jumper for days,
even though it is dirty.
Sometimes she cries in dinners,
even though she is not a little one.
Nobody came to see her in the play,
even though she was Mrs Noah,
and she saw the rainbow first.
At the end of school we run out of the gate like
    marbles,
but slow Jeanie creeps home in inches.

*Rowena Somerville*

# Dreamer

Often the teacher said, 'Dreamer,
Where is your mind today?'
Got cross sometimes and simply said,
'You'll work while others play.'

But still when the rest were scribbling
And the teacher's tongue was still,
He'd idly gaze through the window
At the sun on the singing hill.

And his mind would roam by the mayfield
With the larks all taking flight,
And he'd long to be chasing rabbits
With their tails all flashing white.

Or he'd think of the wooded waters
With the dipper bobbing near,
And he'd long to be plopping pebbles
Where the brook runs fast and clear.

But there's always an end to dreaming —
Or he'd bring on the teacher's rage
So he'd sigh at the dawdling, crawling clock
And return to the puzzling page.

*Eric Finney*

# Some Game

they played the whispering game
told the others
they must make fun of her name
drew pictures of her
passed them round the class
said she smelled
held their noses
when she walked past

and it was just
something they did
just a bit of fun

not their fault
she took it like that

not their fault.

*Joan Poulson*

# And How Was School, Today?

# Home Time

*(after Lorca)*

The afternoon
turns cold.
The classroom windows steam up.

Suddenly
the children playing by the sink
cry out —
through the misted window
the tree at the edge of the playground
has caught fire.
It is growing yellow wings.
Look, teacher, look!  It's flying!

Cold.
With a shiver
the afternoon lies down
on the far side of the playing fields.
It curls up
in a wisp of mist and night.

Pointing golden-apple cheek-red fingers
come from the sky
and tap on the roof-tops.
Quarter past three, they whisper.
Home time.
In the classroom
the teacher lines the children up.

*Brian Morse*

# Behind Bars

Sent back to search for my lost coat,
I shudder in the wintry
evening chill outside locked gates,

grip smooth, cold bars, a prisoner
returning late from his parole,
hope going out with light.

Silence has turned its deadlock round
our school, mist blurs the branches
of our single playground oak

and cramp of iron pains my hands.
Across the chalk of dying sky
starlings in their smoke-plume drift,

billow and fragment.  Their black
blizzard scribbles pages over
darkened roof tops. Their excited

chatter shrills. They shake like pepper
on the tree: its branches over-
spill with wingbeats. Come alive,

the playground swells with squabble.
Spaces between bars and brickwork
fill with clattered mugs and plates on steel
needing night's final warning bell.

*Barrie Wade*

# And How Was School, Today?

Each day they ask: And how was school today?
Behind my mask, I shrug and say OK.

Upstairs, alone, I blink away the tears
Hearing again their scornful jeers and sneers.

Hearing again them call me by those names
As they refused to let me join their games.

Feeling again them mock me with their glares
As they pushed past me rushing down the stairs.

What have I done? Why won't they let me in?
Why do they snigger? What's behind that grin?

Each day they ask: And how was school today?
Behind my mask, I shrug and say OK.

*John Foster*

# Homework! Oh, Homework!

Homework! Oh, homework!
I hate you! You stink!
I wish I could wash you
away in the sink,
if only a bomb
would explode you to bits.
Homework! Oh, homework!
You're giving me fits.

I'd rather take baths
with a man-eating shark,
or wrestle a lion
alone in the dark,
eat spinach and liver,
pet ten porcupines
than tackle the homework,
my teacher assigns.

Homework! Oh, homework!
You're last on my list,
I simply can't see
why you even exist,
if you just disappeared
it would tickle me pink.
Homework! Oh, homework!
I hate you! You stink!

*Jack Prelutsky*

# Homework Tonight

There's homework tonight, so much to be done,
No time for resting, no time for fun!

But first . . .
Something to eat to build up my will power,
Then perhaps a TV programme for half of an hour;
Followed by some music to help me relax
Then a cool drink and a few tasty snacks.

Then it's . . .
Down to studying; give of my best,
Got to work hard; no time to rest.

But first . . .
I'll phone a few friends to see how they are,
Strum a few songs with the help of my guitar;
Switch on the computer — improve my best score,
Try on my new trainers — float across the floor.

Then it's . . .
— *definitely and got to be* —
Down to studying; give of my best,
Got to work hard; no time to rest!

But first . . .
I'll just organize my desk, help with the work load,
Hey! Who's that out the window walking down the road;
Oh and I must check out that film on Thursday night
And back to the fridge to help satisfy my appetite.

Then it's . . .
— *absolutely and definitely and just got to be* —
Down to studying; give of my best,
Got to work hard; no time to rest!

Finally I'm ready, so no further delay,
Sitting at my desk, I'm here to stay;
Now all I need are a pencil and ruler I can borrow,
What! 9 o'clock already — well there's always
    tomorrow!

*Ian Souter*

# Good Girls

Good girls
will always go like clockwork
home from school,

through the iron gates
where clambering boys
whisper and pull,

past houses
where curtains twitch
and a fingery witch beckons,

by the graveyard
where stone angels stir,
itching their wings,

past tunnelled woods
where forgotten wolves wait
for prey,

past dens
and caves and darknesses
they go like clockwork;

and when they come
to school again
their homework's done.

*Irene Rawnsley*

# The Consolation Prize

Far too busy being cool
I never won a thing at school.
Middling was my position
In every kind of competition.

Teachers, thinking they were wise,
Gave me the consolation prize
Which, like a box with nothing in it,
Never fooled me for one minute.

*John Mole*

# Parents' Evening

Parents' evening, parents' evening,
Brings an end to all deceiving,
Parents' evening, parents' evening,
Brings an end to all deceiving.

Parents' evening's coming,
The world is looking black,
My parents think that I've tried hard,
I'd better go and pack.
I tried to hide the letter
But they found it in my bag,
They'll ground me for a month or two,
Isn't life a drag.

Parents' evening, parents' evening,
Brings an end to all deceiving,
Parents' evening, parents' evening,
Brings an end to all deceiving.

Parents' evening's coming,
My survival chance is slim,
I told them I get house points
But the teachers keep me in
For being rude and cheeky,
And for talking at the back,
For occasionally nicking
The odd thing that I lack.

Parents' evening, parents' evening,
Brings an end to all deceiving,

Parents' evening, parents' evening,
Brings an end to all deceiving.

Parents' evening's coming
So I've tried to make amends,
I've apologized to teachers
And treated them like friends.
I've requested the forgiveness
Of those who are so wise,
And asked if they could see their way
To telling a few lies.

Parents' evening, parents' evening,
Brings an end to all deceiving,
Parents' evening, parents' evening,
Brings an end to all deceiving.

Parents' evening's coming
And there's nothing I can do
To change my reputation
In just a day or two.
They'll say they're disappointed,
They expected more of me,
And I'll say that I've been a fool
Not to plainly see that . . .

Parents' evening, parents' evening,
Brings an end to all deceiving,
Parents' evening, parents' evening,
Brings an end to all deceiving.

*Coral Rumble*

# Bad Report — Good Manners

My daddy said, 'My son, my son,
This school report is bad.'
I said, 'I did my best I did,
My dad my dad my dad.'
'Explain, my son, my son,' he said,
'Why *bottom* of the class?'
'I stood aside, my dad my dad,
To let the others pass.'

*Spike Milligan*

# The Test

I'm not looking forward to tomorrow,
For tomorrow we've got the Test.
Mum's told me to try not to worry
And just to do my best.

But I can't get to sleep for wondering
What the questions will be,
And what if my friends all pass and go
To a different school from me.

It's no good pretending I'll ever
Come out top of the class.
I only hope that I get enough marks
To be one of the few who pass.

*John Foster*

# Standing Up to Read a Poem
# In Front of All These People

I've got to do it,
Sir says so,
And we've been practising
For weeks.
We missed games last night,
To have a
Final Rehearsal.
I've got to do it,
Because sir's picked me,
And Mam says she'll be proud,
But sir says NOT TOO LOUD
And don't rush it;
But I feel sure
I'll mess it up.
It'll be all right
If I remember how it should go,
And our Jim doesn't pick his nose,
In the front row,
And make me laugh.
So here goes . . .
. . .
Damn . . .
How does it begin?

*John Cunliffe*

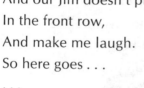

# The Last Boy to School

The last boy to school
counts drifting sheep
between the dreaming clouds.

The last boy to school
follows snails' silver trails
down the slow winding path.

The last boy to school
feels each shade of green
that gleams in the glistening trees.

The last boy to school
sees no need
for the rulers,
the set squares, the text books:

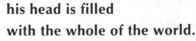

his head is filled
with the whole of the world.

*Dave Ward*

# Index of Titles and First Lines

*First lines are in italics*

# Index of Authors

# Acknowledgements

The editor and publisher are grateful to the following for permission to include poems: **Moira Andrew:** 'No Ordinary Day', Copyright © Moira Andrew 1997, first published here by permission of the author. **Clare Bevan:** 'The Carol Singer', Copyright © Clare Bevan 1997, first published here by permission of the author. **Stephen Bowkett:** 'Donna Didn't Come Back', Copyright © Stephen Bowkett 1997, first published here by permission of the author. **Tony Bradman:** 'Fox' and 'The Boy', Copyright © Tony Bradman 1997, first published here by permission of the author. **Sandy Brownjohn:** 'The Games Lesson' from *Both Sides of the Catflap* (Hodder Children's Books, 1996) reprinted by permission of Hodder & Stoughton Ltd. **John Coldwell:** 'Thirteen Questions You Should be Prepared to Answer if you Lose Your Ears at School', Copyright © John Coldwell 1995, from *Penny Whistle Pete* (Collins, 1995), and 'It's Cold', Copyright © John Coldwell 1992, from *The Slack-Jawed Camel* (Stride, 1992), both reprinted by permission of the author. **Andrew Collett:** 'Please Let Me Stay at Home', Copyright © Andrew Collett 1997, first published here by permission of the author. **Paul Cookson:** 'Teacher's Very Quiet Today' from *The Toilet Seat Has Teeth* (A Twist in the Tale, 1992), Copyright © Paul Cookson 1992, reprinted by permission of the author. **Wendy Cope:** 'Team Spirit', Copyright © Wendy Cope 1997, first published here by permission of the author. **John Cunliffe:** 'Latecomers' and 'Standing up to Read a Poem in Front of All These People', both from *Standing on a Strawberry* (Deutsch), reprinted by permission of David Higham Associates. **Jan Dean:** 'Uniform' from *Nearly Thirteen* (Blackie, 1994), text Copyright © Jan Dean 1994, reprinted by permission of Penguin Books Ltd. **John C. Desmond:** 'Green' and 'Summer', both Copyright © John C. Desmond 1997, first published here by permission of the author. **Berlie Doherty:** 'Quieter than Snow' and 'I'm Telling You', both from *Walking on Air* (HarperCollins), reprinted by permission of Murray Pollinger on behalf of the author. **Helen Dunmore:** Untitled playground haiku from *Secrets* (The Bodley Head), reprinted by permission of Random House UK Ltd. **Eric Finney:** 'Marked' and 'Dreamer', both Copyright © Eric Finney 1997, first published here by permission of the author. **John Foster:** 'Teachers' from *Four O'Clock Friday* (OUP,1991),and 'And How Was School Today?' from *Standing on the Sidelines* (OUP, 1995), both reprinted by permission of Oxford University Press; 'Miss Rodd', 'I Am a Question Mark', and 'The Test', Copyright © John Foster 1997, first published here by permission of the author. **Roy Fuller:** 'A School Mistress called Binks Lies Here' from 'Epitaphs', originally published in *Seen Grandpa Lately?* (Deutsch, 1972), reprinted by permission of John Fuller. **Mick Gowar:** 'New Leaf' first published in *Third Time Lucky* (Penguin), reprinted by permission of the author. **Mike Harding:** 'School Bully' from *Buns for the Elephants* (Viking, 1995), text Copyright © Mike Harding 1995, reprinted by permission of Penguin Books Ltd. **Adrian Henri:** 'Morning Break' from *The Phantom Lollipop Lady and Other Poems* (first published in 1986 by Methuen Children's Books), Copyright © Adrian Henri 1986, reproduced by permission of the author c/o Rogers, Coleridge & White Ltd, 20 Powis Mews, London W11 1JN. **Maggie Holmes:** 'In the Playground' and 'Please Read' from *Pribble Prabble* (Sherbourne Publications, 1992), reprinted by permission of the author. **Elizabeth Honey:** 'Back to School Blues' from *Honey Sandwich* (G. Allen & Unwin). **Mike Jubb:** 'School is Closed Today Because...' and 'Do We Have to Write a Poem